All I need is a little twig,
so why do they make these trees so big?

THE WORLD, CLEVERLY DISGUISED

with poetry and art supplies

Alica Martwick

Lovingly dedicated to my favorite
mixed-media masterpieces,
Josh and Benji

POSSIBILITIES

Stories are told,
space travel plotted,
portraits are drawn
and melodies jotted.

Recipes simmer,
secrets confessed,
gadgets invented,
love is professed.

Heroes and villains and
plans for skyscraper –
a whole world awaits
in a fresh sheet of paper...

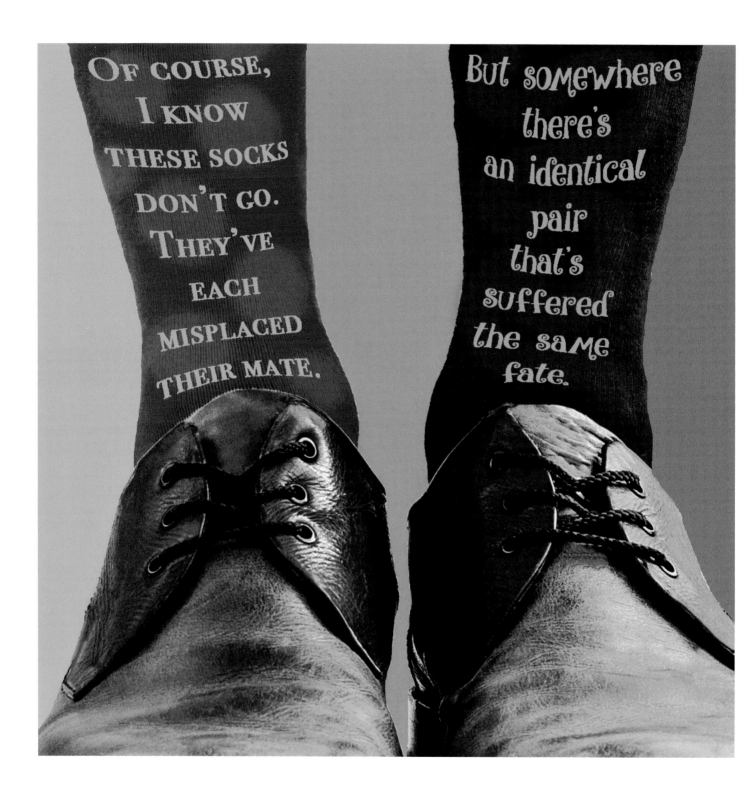

TWO PEOPLE,
GIVEN THE SAME SITUATION,
WILL GIVE BIRTH TO
ENTIRELY DIFFERENT CREATIONS.
OFFERED TWO STICKS
TO RUB TOGETHER,
ONE MAKES A CAMPFIRE,
THE OTHER, A SWEATER.

At the famous PLEATS boutique at the end of Scissor Street,
they'll dress you up in paper from your head down to your feet.
It's true, the clothes are fragile - they can crumple, they can tear -
but you'll never find a shirt more neatly folded anywhere.

i BUILT THIS WALL
THERE IS NO DOUBT
TO KEEP THE FEAR & ANGER
OUT
UNFORTUNATELY
TO MY CHAGRIN
IT ALSO KEEPS THOSE FEELINGS
IN ☹

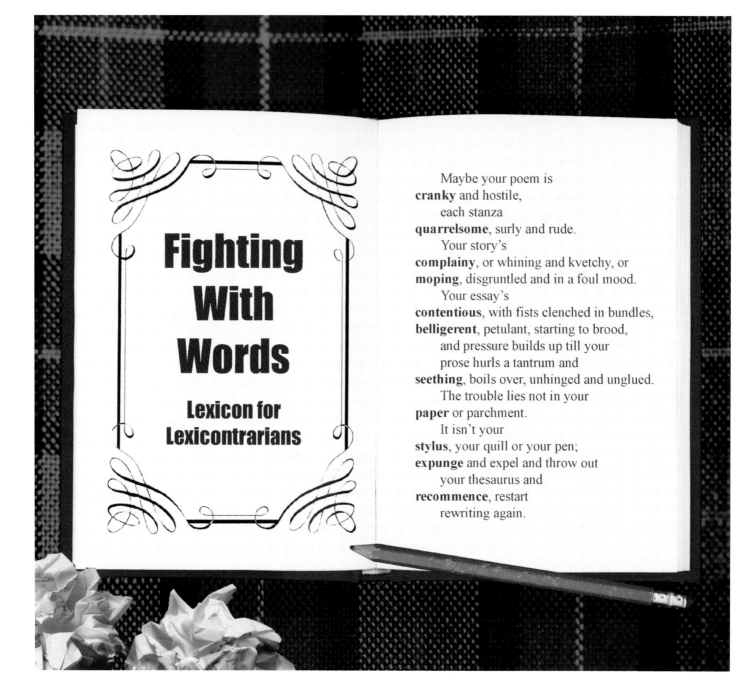

Fighting With Words

Lexicon for Lexicontrarians

Maybe your poem is
cranky and hostile,
each stanza
quarrelsome, surly and rude.
Your story's
complainy, or whining and kvetchy, or
moping, disgruntled and in a foul mood.
Your essay's
contentious, with fists clenched in bundles,
belligerent, petulant, starting to brood,
and pressure builds up till your
prose hurls a tantrum and
seething, boils over, unhinged and unglued.
The trouble lies not in your
paper or parchment.
It isn't your
stylus, your quill or your pen;
expunge and expel and throw out
your thesaurus and
recommence, restart
rewriting again.

I just spent a year
writing haiku every day.
Now I talk like this.

So many things I'd like to do but it seems all I ever do is watch while other people do the many things I'd like to do.

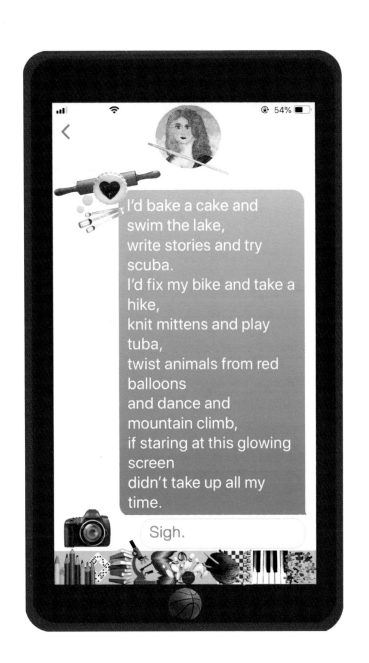

I'd bake a cake and swim the lake,
write stories and try scuba.
I'd fix my bike and take a hike,
knit mittens and play tuba,
twist animals from red balloons
and dance and mountain climb,
if staring at this glowing screen
didn't take up all my time.

Sigh.

Without the help of crystal ball,

The fortune cookie foresees all

And sweeter still, adds twist to caper:

Fits destiny on tiny paper.

No two snowflakes are alike.
No two fingerprints are alike.
Contemplating these two truths
has left me most convinced:
since no two people are alike
and no two snowmen are alike,
it stands to reason snowflakes
must be snowman fingerprints.

And now that you've considered
all the cold hard evidence,
I'm sure that you'll agree:
this logic simply makes snow sense.

One plays a solo.
Duets come in pairs.
Trios play in threeO's,
and quartets play in squares.
Quintets play in star-shapes,
and sextets play in hexagons,

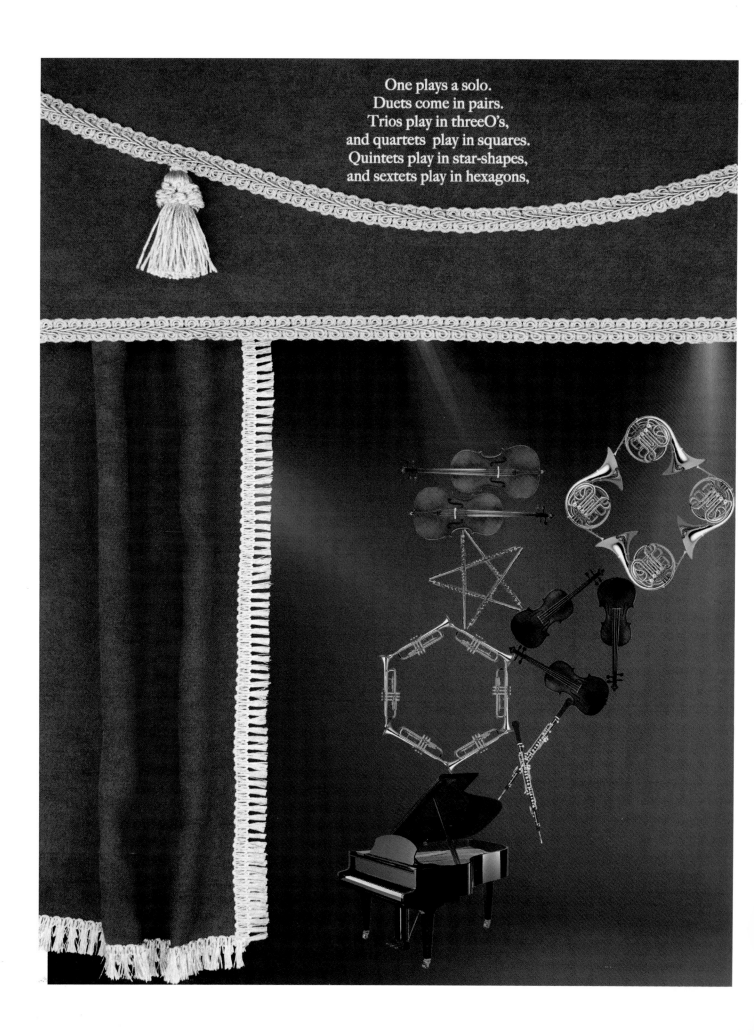

and symphony orchestras
play in googolplexagons.

Headfirst is the only way to dive into a good book.

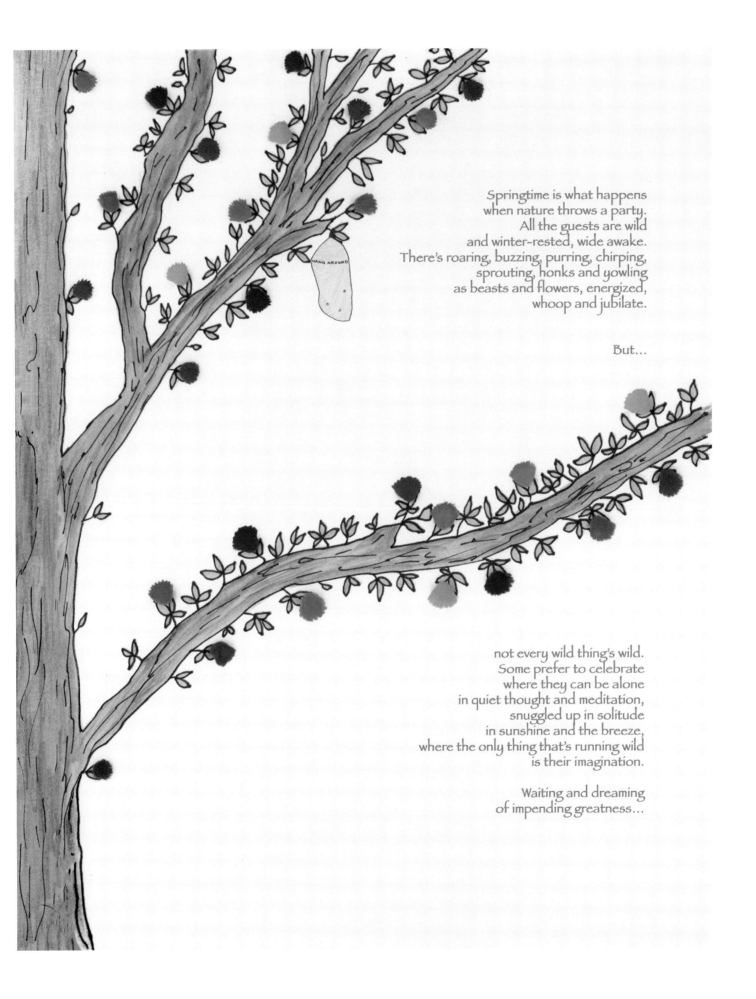

Springtime is what happens
when nature throws a party.
All the guests are wild
and winter-rested, wide awake.
There's roaring, buzzing, purring, chirping,
sprouting, honks and yowling
as beasts and flowers, energized,
whoop and jubilate.

But…

not every wild thing's wild.
Some prefer to celebrate
where they can be alone
in quiet thought and meditation,
snuggled up in solitude
in sunshine and the breeze,
where the only thing that's running wild
is their imagination.

Waiting and dreaming
of impending greatness…

ODE DEAR

There once lived a poet who loved a fair maiden
with love only poems could prove.
He attempted to woo her with heartfelt haiku,
but the maiden remained unmoved.

Her brush-off so scornful left poor poet mournful,
his usual ruddiness pallid.
So, he picked up his pen and set sail again
and wrote her a meaningful ballad.

The maid, unimpressed, left poet distressed.
He resorted to show-offy gimmick –
in desperate pursuit and without parachute,
he composed an embarrassing limerick.

The maid said, "I'd give you my hand if I knew
you could speak from your heart without rhyming."
The poet sighed deeply, looked into her eyes,
and said, "OK, I can do that."

Home is wherever you can let your true colors show

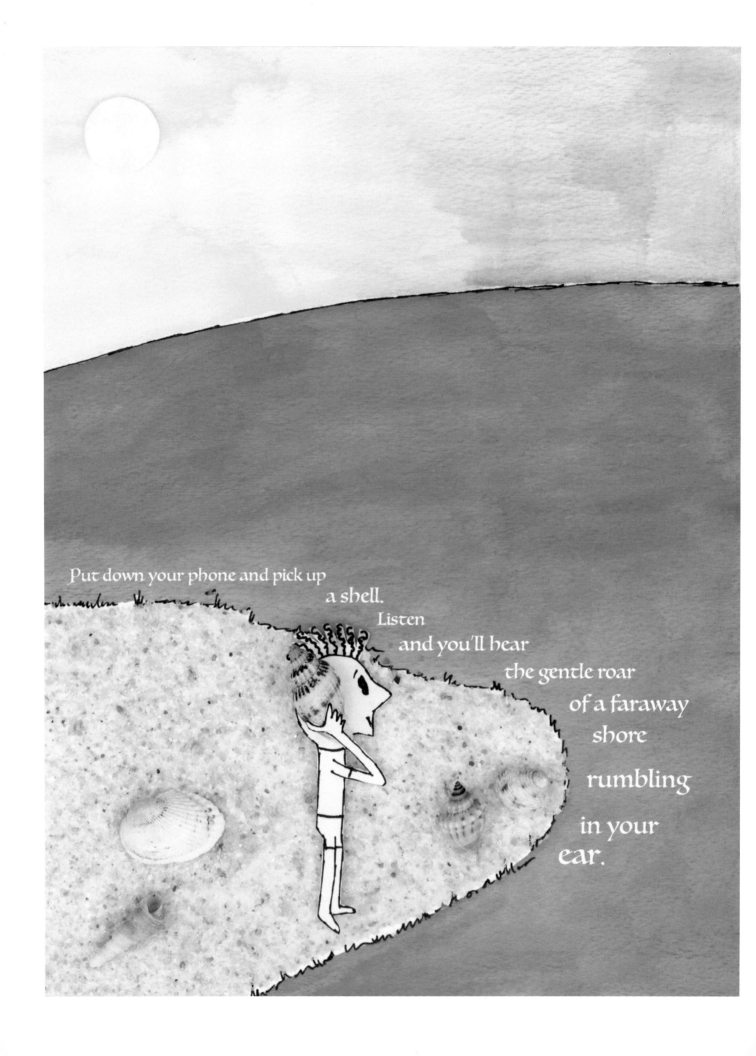

Put down your phone and pick up a shell. Listen and you'll hear the gentle roar of a faraway shore rumbling in your ear.

You've
    reached somebody
            just like you
                    on the beach
        of a distant land,
            who hears the roar
                    of your seashore
        in the seashell in her hand.

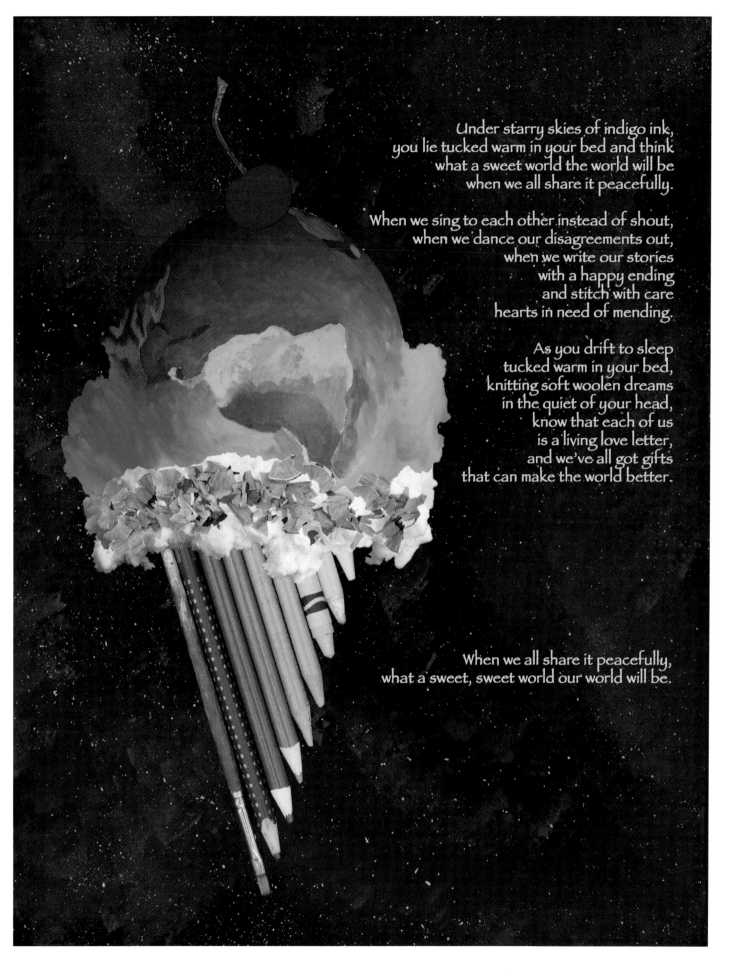

Under starry skies of indigo ink,
you lie tucked warm in your bed and think
what a sweet world the world will be
when we all share it peacefully.

When we sing to each other instead of shout,
when we dance our disagreements out,
when we write our stories
with a happy ending
and stitch with care
hearts in need of mending.

As you drift to sleep
tucked warm in your bed,
knitting soft woolen dreams
in the quiet of your head,
know that each of us
is a living love letter,
and we've all got gifts
that can make the world better.

When we all share it peacefully,
what a sweet, sweet world our world will be.

Special thanks to special people:

To Brett Sherman, photographer cleverly disguised as transistor builder...

to my creative confidantes, Doranne Awad, Barbara Bartzi, Lynnette Hardy,
Laurie Kelsoe, Marianne McCanta, Diane McKean, Holly Munly, T.L. Murray,
Kathleen Orrick, Sheri Perry, Sandy Rosenberg, Suzanne Schoenfeld, Kim Sherman,
Meagan Silva and Relly Weltman, for their helpful feedback and patient encouragement...

to DaFont, Freepik and GoGraph, for assorted artistic elements...

and to Andy, for everything.

FROM THE AUTHOR

I have had many different jobs.
I was a press secretary, a technical editor,
I worked in social services, and I edited songs that played on
modern-day old-timey player pianos. I always carried with me a little
notebook in which I jotted down ideas for stories and songs
that I hoped to someday write and art I hoped to someday create,
and I'm delighted to finally be writing and creating.
I now try to work on creative projects every day.

Thank you for reading my book!
:-) Alica